For Hannah,

with much love.

x x

Stu

13/11/17

Shooting Stars

Saúl Díaz Reales

S.

Translation: *Saúl Díaz Reales / Danielle Reales.*

Editing: *Nora Aridi / Danielle Reales.*

Cover design: *Danielle Reales.*

ACKNOWLEDGEMENTS

This book contains a compilation of short stories translated from my three previous books, originally published in Spanish, as well as some yet unpublished stories. It would have never been possible without the help of Danielle and Nora. I am eternally grateful.

For more information, please visit my website

www.sauldiazreales.com

"And the end of all our exploring
Will be to arrive where we started
And know the place for the first time."

T S Eliot
"Little Gidding"

"Lost time is never found again."

Benjamin Franklin
"Poor Richard's Almanac"

Dedicated to our little nieces:
María, *Laura* and *Rocío*,
for always greeting us
with so much happiness.

INDEX

IF I SHOULD CHOOSE

If I should choose to stay... Would you promise to love me? To sleep by my side, snuggled on my shoulder, breathing the air of our kisses, the warmth of our bed...

If you chose to love me... Would you promise to tell me so every morning? When you open your eyes and see me by your side, gazing at you, watching your pupils adjust to the light and you dedicate to me your first smile, your first yawn, your first kiss, your first breath of the new day's air.

If you should choose to tell me that you love me... Would you promise to love me forever? When I am happy and when I am sad. When I behave strangely at times, when I cry for yesterday, when I ask for your forgiveness, when I unthinkingly annoy you. When I say things that make no sense, when I don't understand the moment; when my questions about love hover all around us, and amongst them a single answer lands on your chest shouting that what we feel is real, that it will transcend even after our lives have been extinguished, echoing throughout all eternities.

And if you chose to promise to love me forever... Would you also promise to make me feel it at every opportunity? When you catch me staring at you, when I look into your eyes. When I search for your embrace, when I tell you that I do love you. When I forget to remember that I must not be afraid.

FAREWELL

My last memory of you is still trapped in our last embrace. My last remembrance of what we were, in that past that is now gone, is still frozen in a file of memories, immune to time, distance and all the interferences I have experienced ever since. The two of us, quietly sharing a silence both tender and tearful, embracing one another. Our bodies transmitting warmth, helplessness and rage; feeling every ounce of love that we were allowed to share within the fugacious time our destinies walked the same path. Reticent tears swelling in our eyes, no desire to part, no instinct to escape, no yearning to unchain wailings that would make our farewell even more bitter. Meanwhile, new worlds were born, and many others perished, to continue a cycle in which we as one would cease to exist. The fabric of darkness constricted the space around us emitting abhorrent screeches, searing the air, extinguishing the oxygen, annihilating all the smiles that until that day we had dedicated to one another.

I close my eyes and I see myself in that embrace, in that instant in which the sorrow looked patiently at its watch. I live it; I am there with you again. We both know this is a farewell as defined by a dictionary, a farewell that does not permit that we ever meet again. We know it, and for this reason we do not allow our tears to fall. I wish we could stop time. I wish we could stay forever in this embrace, in utter silence, with tears flooding our eyes, sobbing. Our skin electrified and our hearts beating as one, saying goodbye to each other as we said goodbye, knowing that there would be no after, and that all that will exist between them now is an infinite distance, pain and void. I wish we could stop time, how I wish we could, while the world continues, disintegrates and is reborn from nothingness.

I would have wanted to keep you in my life, at least, as a friend. For your company was always pleasant. The stars we named on those nights at the beach are my witnesses. My fears were always milder when shared with you. Peace seemed more conceivable, more tangible and imminent with each and every hug. I would have wanted to have more time to learn from you, to know your dreams, to have helped you achieve them. I would have wanted to know what it is about the dark that frightens you, to be able to defeat it so you could sleep more peacefully. But we knew that this rupture had to be merciless, without looking back. The risk of turning into statues of salt was too great to be ignored.

My plane awaits. The plane that will carry me to the other side of the ocean, to the place where I was born, to hide me for a thousand eternities; to deny the Sun and the stars; to renounce everything, even you. My plane awaits, like cruelty awaits its time to hurt, to rip souls apart leaving wounds that will never heal, to break apart what magic once brought together in the hope that it would last, even when our lives had come to an end.

My plane awaits like my tears wait to flow from my eyes in a futile attempt to empty the hurt that I now feel; like the executioner waits to extinguish a life with one accurate blow. Our paths will drift apart forever. You will find new lovers, new experiences, a part of which I will never be. Time will soften what we now feel, making us believe that it was something of the moment, transient and ephemeral... How naive! Some day, I know, we will remember that time with a smile. But on that day there will still be a feeling of doubt, a question with no answer, about what could have been. For the answer was denied to us even before we had the need to ask.

My last memory of you is still trapped in our last embrace.

MY HEART

My heart has died again today. Its heartbeats, withered echoes from the past, keep hammering the walls in my chest, as if trying to escape from its prison, as if wishing to fully die, at once, forever. Its movements, painting overtones on the canvas of the now, carry on driven by the inertia of the days gone by.

My eyes, sad mirrors of extinguished happiness, are again flooded with the salty tears of uncertainty. My pupils, always willing to look beyond the impossible, are now covered with heavy eyelids, with a curtain of sorrow that allows no light through the gloom. My face, once before full of dreams, practices the gestures of the most inhuman hurt.

The room seems to shrink, tightening the air, describing the most infinite of distances: the one that exists only because we both want it to exist. The memory of what once had been, curses itself for not saying, for not knowing, for not ripping to shreds the space that separates the bodies of these two lovers, now hurt, bruised, numbed by a frost that understands no promises or wandering heartbeats. The cruel destiny inhabits a present that should be ornamented with a thousand I-love-yous. The kisses we do not give to each other float in the ether, while our eager lips desperately pursue them, realising they are impossible to catch.

Outside, unraveling in the sky of the gloomy sunset, storm clouds electrify the air threatening hurricanes that will devastate the prairies where snow had only yesterday drawn landscapes of hope and new joy. The rain falls slowly, exterminating the scent of the flowers that were awaiting the morning Sun. Fallen leaves rot amongst the undergrowth.

The smell of emptiness fills the space that should be full of warm embraces.

Meanwhile she weeps, emptying her sorrows and burning the skin on her cheeks. She tries to speak, but can only utter sobs that rip unintentionally another piece of my soul. The heart in my chest beats with fury. Meanwhile she cries tearing apart the fabric of everything that exists, longing for solace, attempting to comprehend what is really happening. Meanwhile she also feels her heart slowly dying, once again.

There are things from the past that are best left behind.

ON THE URBAN TRAIN

People scattered, located in random positions, dragged by their whims. Each immersed in their thoughts, in their problems, in their fears… Dozens of empty eyes, all so full of loneliness.

The fifth dimension appears behind the reflection in the window. Another reality, following the laws of parallel universes, appears eerily in between the dance of lights and shadows.

I take myself in there, into the dimension behind the window. Here the empty stares take on another meaning. Here they meet, taking on other tones, other hues and complicity. Here we all know each other, and we all share that hope of a better world. It is our unreal moment, our momentary hideout. Our way of communication, in a society of people isolated within themselves, protected by the armour of an iPod.

It is possible to dance behind the mirror together with the person sitting next to you. Perhaps, whispering verses in the ear of that girl, whose eyes are plagued by a curtain of sorrow; to take the wrinkled hand of that little old lady and tell her, just by moving our lips, that we will keep fighting for her when her strength departs…

The driver announces by loud speaker that we are approaching our destination. We hasten to finish the dance, embrace in a final hug, and we wish each other luck. We return to our own bodies, in which we do not know each other. The train stops. Doors open, and we continue our hectic race to I don't know where…

THREE POEMS

I

Your absence is that overtone of my loneliness that defines the fire that consumes me.

The longest hours are endless when the clock, the impatient clock, ticks in your absence.

The bitterness I am accustomed to, even more invades my eyes, tired from a search that only finds vanishing mirages.

My voice, silent and resigned, died on that very moment in which your last kiss whispered to me that goodbye.

II

My soul is exhausted from sailing through empty deserts in which you are not. Never had waiting been so long.

The corners of this space, which you do not inhabit, have no understanding of time other than to increase that melancholy of mine that not even you have ever met.

The days of apathy delay the movements of the hands in my clock, in a cruel game that no one comprehends.

The spells of the minutes passing by, of the over stretched hours, are my routine and the source of my deep sadness.

I die slowly in this dark pit in which I have made my home until you arrive.

III

A shooting moment landed on my window, as if suddenly arrived, like a voice in the vacuum. It brought me olive tree branches, and such beautiful songs.

A flaming thunder peeped at my balcony. It took my hand, caressing it. It gave me its time, it gave me its lips, and left again.

An enchanted flower flew to my side, opened its petals, gave me its smile. It left its perfume on my sheets, it left its fingerprints in my corner.

A wandering whisper defeated me, spoke in my ear, sang me tales and lullabies. It broke my long lived lethargy.

A rain of kisses caught me off guard, in that very moment in which all is silent.

WALK

Walk. Look forward. Head up, your goal: the horizon. Engrave it in your mind. Let your gestures be calm, drawing in the invisible ether symbols of a language long forgotten by man.

Do not hesitate: for everything and every situation you will find a thousand ways. So before you, only the truth should prevail. Learn a lesson from each experience you encounter on your way. Analyse it and reach your own truth. It is paramount to know the land you roam, the orbit in which you rotate, the true value of your beliefs. But be aware that your truth, may well be deviated from *the* truth. So question it. For the truth must be free from exceptions. Above all, preach only by example. Remember that the world does not revolve around you and while you observe and meticulously scrutinize the actions of others, likewise others are observing and analysing your own.

Talk: for words can defeat a thousand barbarous armies and reason shall continue to be victorious over any confrontation. Speak the language of tenderness and understanding, but do not hesitate to sharpen your tongue when the situation demands it. There is much quackery, many empty words spoken from ignorance. Do not fear to ask what you do not know: a single moment of ignorance is a step towards a life of wisdom. Open yourself to those who enquire with a good heart. Help others to get where you have arrived, however much you have left to go.

Do not look back: there is no value in spying on the footprints imprinted in the road that has been traveled. The horizon is more stunning, more disturbing and unknown. Sometimes it is framed by a rainbow, that invites you to increase your pace, creating the illusion that you may caress it with your fingertips. However beware: it is just a beautiful mirage. But if you still choose to look back, be ready to meet The Past, for a sheer gaze shall give it permission to gain momentum in an attempt to join with the present. It is highly dangerous to live today with the echoes of yesterday, for in the end they shall only serve to condition our existence. Memories of better times shall eventually become ghosts that dwell within us, urging us to believe that such moments are never to return. My advice to you is to live the now squeezing every second, so as to avoid having to remember the past for comfort. Learn to live so that you may never suffer the grief that remains after a bad deed has been executed. Do not create ghosts that may pursue you. And do not delay in becoming aware that, no matter how you use your time, the ticking clock is indifferent.

Follow the trail of light: you will recognize it because it is surrounded by shadows. For the eternal duality of everything is present everywhere you look. Do not put your hopes in higher beings, for nothing is more powerful than you. Now, guided by respect, place all your efforts in reaching your goals. Follow the path of light, the one surrounded by shadows, the one your heart guides you to follow, and believe strongly that at the end of the trail, you will find what has always been there, waiting for you. Such is the power of this, our Universe, to create our own reality, our own way beyond the light, even beyond the horizon.

Be happy: in whichever way you believe best defines your own concept of happiness. To do this, you must know yourself, know who you are, what you defend, what you oppose, what you want, and more importantly, what you do not want. Do not evaluate your happiness based on other individuals', for happiness cannot be measured, it is no more than nor less than; it is intimate and personal, an energy state at another quantum level. For happiness is, in itself, the very pursuit of happiness.

Above all, be compassionate: this is the hope of the human race. Let your actions be guided by your inner being: help the needy without expecting something in return, other than their commitment to also help others. For this shall be the seed that permeates throughout the world, man to man, person to person, selflessly, with the sole intention of spreading the Great Activity, the brotherhood that we, all human beings, are. Let your ways be fair, as you must understand that everyone, including yourself, commits mistakes, and sometimes anger temporarily defeats us. For it is the frequent loss of this battle that transforms men into abominations.

Sleep well: nothing is more restful than sleeping with a clear conscience. Each night you may visit that place where the Memory of the Cosmos is stored, of which every being that ever existed is a part of. You will hear the prayers and praises of those who are, and hear the stories of those who have been. Learn the wisdom of those who attained enlightenment. And do not forget to thank the new day on waking up, for giving you a new opportunity to do good, to be able to witness again the orange hues of another sunset, the scent of the flowers that, like you, give thanks to the new day for awakening the Sun from its nocturnal sleep.

Move ahead, walk, find the reason for your own existence. Look forward. Head up, your goal: the horizon. Engrave it in your mind. Let your gestures be calm, drawing in the invisible ether symbols of a language long forgotten by man...

TOMORROW

I care not who the ruler is nor who the captain might be, for tomorrow I walk again the path that leads to where she awaits. Today I care not about the battle nor the motive, for my compass already points to her arms, to her body, to her love songs and her kisses. She is the magnetic north that guides the birds on their way back to the summer, escaping from the frost and the snow, from cold winds and hurricanes. Like I, now escape from the distance, to return to her.

Today I care not about my fortune, about mighty storms or my fears. My destiny is already imprinted on the pages of the almanac, and nothing can alter it. The rain has fallen in my absence, tattooing on my chest poems that speak of love, words of hope and scents of eternal dreams. That same rain has left behind a rainbow that ends on her lips. The sails of my ship, unfurled to infinity, capture the new aft wind. The helm is fixed on a straight line towards the woman I love. It matters not how long I have ventured into the distance: I have not been anywhere until I have returned home.

Tomorrow I start the journey to where I long to be. Tomorrow another story will be written about my heart reuniting with my beloved's. We shall be one again tomorrow, our chests will beat together again, beaming waves of undefeatable power, erasing the melancholy we have been drowned in during the eternity that kept us apart, speaking only with the echo of the last words we said to each other. The sea shall be calm, and the heavens will shine blue like her eyes. The Moon will stay longer in the sky to guide my steps during my farewell.

For tomorrow it will be a new day, a new Sun and a new awakening. A new day, and not just another day. Tomorrow I will return to her embrace, like the smiles return after the tears, like spring returns after the withering winter, like the dark swallows return each and every year.

Tomorrow brings the time in which I will awake again by her side. I will gaze at her as she sleeps, smell her perfume and give her my warmth. Tomorrow we will be together again, picking up dreams right where we left them, defining the words to express our feelings so that they will not remain unsaid, as so many important things are.

Tomorrow the last day ends, but the first day begins. Tomorrow I return to her laughter and her company, to her tenderness and her affection. Tomorrow I will see her impatient eyes waiting, witnessing that what I wrote in my letters is true. She will cry when she sees me, and from each and every tear there will be a new star that she will name after a flower. For tomorrow it will be the birth of a new constellation.

MY BELOVED

The day starts with a kiss. A soft caress brings me out of my lethargy. I look at your blue eyes, your red hair, your gentle smile. I reach out to hold you, and you do the same. We stay like that, in an eternal moment in which there is no time, no lights, no wars. Not even the songbirds are given the chance to fill space with their music. My hands can feel the warmth flowing from every pore of your skin. Blue sparks timidly flicker in fleeting moments. I smell your hair and I know you are real.

We walk holding hands through beautiful gardens, where flowers bloom for us to see. I pick the most precious one and offer it to you. You accept it, and place it in your hair. Squirrels stop leaping through the trees to admire the aura of happiness that surrounds us. Water flows silently from a spring. We drink from it, tasting the dew that travelled through the air into the Earth.

Lying on the grass, we pull petals from daisies; the last one always whispers we love each other. All of the clovers have four tiny perfect leaves. In the sky, soft orange clouds play with their shapes to entertain us. At times, they rain droplets of water scented with jasmine. They glide, like snowflakes, to land on your neck.

We return home, walking hand in hand. Our shadows follow, dancing patiently around our unrushed amble. In our home there is no darkness: our doors and windows are always open; the breeze fills every corner with its perfume smelling of east, west, north and south. For it is in our home where the four winds converge. Music fills the space, painting the air with staves and notes that appear with every heartbeat. We slow dance and our feet levitate from the ground. We kiss at every turn as we float higher and higher.

Suddenly, I open my eyes and it was just a dream. I curse the morning for waking me up. I curse the Sun for rising again. I start the day without wanting to live it. I wish to sleep again, to dream again of my beloved. I close my eyelids very tight, but reality has made me its prisoner, torturing my wakefulness. I have no strength to face the hours without her. I do not belong to this side of the mirror, to this wounding awareness, to this nonsense that destroys dawns and haunts the living. Be damned the punishment of living awake in this insane world where happiness is only an illusion, fugacious moments that last only as long as a smile takes to fade. I want to go back to my love, in that world of dreams where we exist together, we belong together, where only her and I live, where tenderness is palpable. I wonder if death would be like that. And I wish to be dead to dream forever.

The hours go by and at last the Moon appears in the night sky. The Sun hides beyond the horizon and I wish for it never to return. I lay on my bed and close my eyes. I let my awareness fade into the oneiric dimension where soon I will meet my beloved again.

I WOULD LIKE

I would like you to be honest. Sincere with me always. Truthful, as so often I did not have the courage to be.

I would like you to love yourself, to wear your hair and your clothing in any style you feel comfortable with. I would like you to realize that it is not necessary to look at your reflection in every mirror to know that you are the most beautiful woman wherever you may be, for your presence never goes unnoticed.

I would like you to understand that all the fears and joys that are important to you, are equally so for many other people. In understanding this, you would not feel any more important than any other person, whatever the circumstances. For in the depths of our being, even without realizing it, we all dream of happiness and of a world without suffering; and at the core of it, we are all equal. I would like you to love others in the same way as your new found love for yourself. You would then comprehend that the world is a beautiful place.

I would like you to feel compassion for all of those who suffer; for you to be moved by the pain of all those mothers who, without understanding why, nor deserving of it, have to see their children dying in their arms, their bodies filled with shrapnel, bullet holes and blood, their eyes lost in the infinite, dry from dust and death. Such a tragic outcome of one of many wars in the name of religion, oil and money. Wars that are always initiated by the powerful, by those who would never send their sons to fight and die. I would like that feeling to fill you with the strength to act, forbidding injustices to be carried out in your name, driving you to stand against any abuse in your presence, and to always act in favour of the hardest hit, of the weaker, of whom they were trying to oppress, of the poor little soul.

I would like you to understand that truth is relative, and that every person is entitled to understand the Universe in their own way, those who are right and those of us who are wrong; that good and evil exist only in precise contexts of space and time: what is right is right here and now, and not necessarily anywhere else or tomorrow; that wisdom is not granted to us by life and years alone, but by the analysis of each experience. We all have fears, but if we support each other we could be the bravest. If this is felt on the inside, truly and with no doubts, then there would be nothing we could not achieve, nothing we could not be. For that is the real secret of this, our Universe.

I would like you to use physical force only to restrain those who you would like to tickle, and that after hearing their stories and opinions, you kissed your opponents to death. I would prefer that you never raised your voice other than to exclaim that you are happy; that you were respectful of all opinions, even of those you have not yet come to understand; that in your battles and debates there were never losers, but only new friends. May the power of words assist you in your journey to a better world, and may you learn over time to have compassion for people single-minded and intolerant of any other points of view, for they have not yet learned that it is alright to be wrong. I would like you to persevere, every day, even rebelling against yourself, in becoming a better person.

I would also like you to enjoy playing for the sake of playing, no matter who won the game. For in a game, like in life itself, you can lose even without having made any mistakes. I want you to understand that there is no sense in worrying, as there is a dividing line between what has and what has not a solution. If you live your life focusing on what makes you feel good, there is nothing you cannot do, because these feelings align your atoms with the pulse of the cosmos, opening the doors of the place where your desires live.

I would like you to see the bright side of everything that happens to you. That you lived knowing that what is being presented as something negative is nothing but an encouragement, a sign that reality hands to you to push you to chase your dreams. And although at first you might not understand why, it is but a matter of time until the reasons become clear to you. That you had the certainty that above the grey, dark and cloudy sky, the Sun shines bright and beautiful.

I would like you to be passionate, to look forward to tomorrow, but without taking it for granted; to live the present as if your last day was the day after tomorrow. To question it all. I would prefer that you did not let time deceive you with truths that are only old lies, but that you used your intelligence to doubt, contrast and draw your own conclusions. And yet, that you were ready to doubt again when your conclusions were obsolete or proven in error.

I would like you to appreciate the beauty in everything around you. Only seeing the good in every person, in everything, in every feeling. I would like you to be thrilled by sunsets, rainbows, the sound of the rain, the glow of the full Moon, the smell of the wet earth, the flashing brightness of the stars on a clear night, the capricious flight of the butterflies, the hypnotic dancing of the waves in the sea.

I would like you to love me and that you made me feel it every day, at least for a while. That your touch made me vibrate with mixed emotions. That your tears, like your laughter, were sweet and contagious. That you were happy, even if it meant abandoning me for someone else. That the day you did not love me anymore you would not conceal it. I would like you to be ruthless with me that day, regardless of my feelings or of the dark pit where I could become trapped. For your happiness would be the most important to me.

I would like to meet you, see your face, smell the perfume of your body. But meanwhile, you will be a chat window on the internet and I'll keep hoping that you are how I would like you to be.

IT WOULD BE NICE

It would be nice if we all slept peacefully, with no remorse, or worries enslaving us to insomnia. It would be nice to wake up in the morning, to a new day, rested, with renewed will to live and to breathe in the perfume of all the flowers. We could then be grateful, and thank the Sun for illuminating the darkness, taking care not to offend the Moon, for she represents another type of beauty. We would then proceed to step out onto the balcony and smile to the songs of the birds, inhale our first breath of fresh air, yawn and stretch.

It would be nice if we dedicated more time to admire the beauty of the night sky. Lying on our rooftops, freeing our imagination to travel through the Milky Way. It would be nice if shooting stars lasted more than an instant, offering us time to make a wish on every one of them. It would be nice if we truly wished.

It would be nice if we all smiled more, and from deeper within, releasing the magic emitted from our lips. For within us all, even those who are oblivious to it, the entire power of the Universe exists, all the Energy that once created Matter, all the Consciousness that once was free and conspired to create us.

It would be nice if we were in harmony. If we could understand one another to sort out any conflicts using reason. If we had an understanding of everything, always guided by peace and the determination to build a better world for ourselves and for generations to come, despite the separation by centuries of space-time. It would be nice if our selfishness was not the cause of our extinction. If we looked after the planet just like we look after our own homes. For we are all a part of it and should be grateful for its existence.

It would be nice if we could queue with respect. If we opened doors for others. If we respected our elders, always understanding that an elderly person can also be wrong. It would be nice if we offered our seat to a pregnant lady, a disabled person, or to someone in worse health than ourselves. It would be nice if there was no money. If the exchange token was time. If no one was independent, but if all became aware that we all depend on one another. It would be the beginning of the Great Brotherhood of all sentient beings.

It would be nice if children could still play on the streets. If they ran away on seeing the police make their way to scold them. It would be nice if they could walk home from school and we didn't have to build statues called "The Children Playing" as a reminder of a time that was and that will never again be.

It would be so very nice...

A SORROW

There is a sorrow in my chest that prevents me from breathing, rips apart pieces of who I am, and with a smile devours them. There is a thorn in my gut that fills my eyes with tears when I seek your comfort and you are not with me. There is a nail burning in my soul that will not allow me to be myself, to express what I now feel, nor live my last day. There was a hope that left for far away, clouding the curtains of my window, not allowing me to ever see the Sun again.

There is a kiss that I lost and refuses to touch my lips, though I ask, though I implore... There is a light now turned off that condemns me to darkness, when all I long to hear are your tender loving words. There is a plug in my ears that makes me deaf to the songs of the birds, to the music and sounds of the dawn. My soul is so tired, my body so sore. Again I seek you, and yet you are not there.

There is a Hell in my memory that refuses to be defeated, that does not understand, nor dance, nor laugh again, but destroys the spell of what I would like it to be. There is a fire that does not burn, but becomes stronger each time I stare into the mirror, as it extinguishes the reflection of what I once was. There is a cloud in my throat, choking me to sheer silence. It rains acid that hurts like indifference, incomprehension and longing. There are storms in my mind, there is poison in my arteries, there are planets that do not rotate nor have moons or gravity.

There is a dark night in my words that seems to never reach its dawn. There are termites in my body that have built tunnels through the ice. There are ghosts in my eyes, horrible monsters in my dreams. There are nettles on my pillow that will not refrain from stinging me.

There are more days than I want, because without you everything is eternal. There are more hours than minutes, more minutes than seconds, and more desolation than forests. There are more deserts than grasslands, more petals than flowers, more screeches than affection in the manuscript of my destiny. There is more radiation than bombs, more dead bodies than cemeteries, there is more disappointment than love, more tears than rivers that run to the sea.

I am here in the exile of the kisses that do not reach me, of the embraces that I miss, of the whispers that will not raise their voices. I am again far from everything, while everything goes on, indifferently. There is an echo from these walls that haunts me with its continuity, monotonously repeated a thousand times, engraving itself with a chisel in my heart. And I seek and do not find you. And I call you and you do not notice. And I love you and you don't love me back. And I kiss you and you move away. The I-love-yous you say today are only peals of random letters that form words purely by accident.

There is a soreness in my eyes that forces me to feel my sentence. There is a horse at my door that never lets me ride. There is a thief of holes that appears whenever I dig, leaving behind on his departure sand mountains that make even taller the walls of my prison. There is a forget that refuses to make caves in my memory, to dust the spider webs from the unreachable corners. There are disturbing nightmares, there are a thousand questions in the air; there are many full stops, but no sentences to finish. There are penances without crosses and a thousand screeching chains; there is a lot of death in the days that I do not reach your comfort, and only words of salt.

MY CLOCK

I topped up my clock with time so that it could forever pulsate for the eternity that I long to live by your side; so it would engrave our moments in the vastness of space. Its beating, unnoticeable when you are with me, reverberates, ripping my soul, through the emptiness left by your absence. For time, my love, is the language of the silence that annihilates everything when we are apart.

I found you in that place where the earth meets the sky; where the rainbow begins, where hope seeks refuge; where I never dared search for anything for fear of finding something. Before you, my clock only killed seconds, turned present into past, discarded moments just as they were created.

I charged my clock with time to allow for these moments with you to be ageless, so as to hurry without rushing towards the future in your arms. I emptied the doubts from my pockets; I stuffed your pillow with poems while you were adding labels to my wishes, painting our home with autumn leaves, composing the music, awaiting my lyrics. I abandoned my impatience when you lent your soul to me.

I cooled my clock with snow, slowing down the movement of its hands. I bent its cogs with fire so that each minute would last forever. I wrapped your body in my arms, whispering my dreams to you, as your eyes traced my lips. I lost the key to your bedroom, cuddling up in your sheets, and I dreamt of you.

I met you in that place where dreams are just dreams; where the night dissolves the shadows. I tore from my calendar the months that were not Spring.

I wound my clock with time so that moments with you stood still, so that the thens became nows, for together we are stronger than each one of us apart. I trapped your time in my clock so that our future was made up of everything that never existed in our past, so that its hands painted our destiny of shared dreams. I filled my clock with our dreams so that your smile never faded. For time may wrinkle and age our bodies, but can never kill our souls.

OUR EMBRACE

Even long before it was consummated, that embrace of ours, our embrace, was condemned never to interfere with destiny. Like the brief existence of a snowflake that disintegrates as it reaches the ground, changing its physical state, turning into water, our embrace, beautiful and strong, transformed instantly into the tears of what will never ever again be. The feelings that laid the foundations of this embrace were eternally relegated to a different future, maybe one in a parallel reality, in which you and I would forever long repeat this moment for many eternities.

Like a rainbow, whose beauty is cursed to fade as it ceases to rain, that will never be part of something greater, the only feature of our embrace was not that we cared for each other but rather the culmination of all the little things that, before it, happened between us. There is no sadder embrace than the one which implies no future, no further hugs nor caresses, not even another kiss. This sad embrace was our embrace.

I would have made time stand still so that your arms would have surrounded my body forever, so that your warmth and mine would have remained always as one, so that the scent of your perfume forever filled the air around us. But time, that bandit that is unconcerned for lovers and for eternal moments, charged on forward indifferently. As it did so, your arms began to forget mine, fabricating a distance between our hearts that grew as we started to forget. I would have tried to enchant you with my poems, singing softly into your ear the songs that I wrote for you, telling you again that my heart was yours, although my lips, overwhelmed by the emotion, couldn't help but tremble.

With a final glance, you built a wall between us and destroyed all hope with your farewell. With every step that you drew away from me, you erased the story that could have been.

And that was our last time. You left me with the broken shards of a dream that I dared to dream without your permission, where my bed was your bed, where my life was yours. You left me with tears that dried before I cried them, with a new scar in my pain that no word has since been able to describe. And I was left alone, with the echo of your presence, watching the distance between us widen as you moved away, taking away everything, even the memory of that kiss that I once stole from you.

In that embrace I loved you and could have sworn you loved me too. How foolish of me! What was no more than an instant could not have left a more engraved memory than that which these words now express.

PERISHABLE

Tonight, for me, all the stars could be blackened, the Moon erased and the Sun extinguished...

For tonight I'm with you and with no one else, together, embraced. I feel the warmth of your body invading my clothes and blending with mine. And nothing can make this moment more beautiful. We raise our foreheads. My lips feel your breath tickling my face. We tighten our embrace, feeling this unique moment, unlike all the previous moments, and certainly unlike those to come, forging, becoming alive, taking shape from tonight. Let the tears of sorrow be dried, the groans of pain, the loneliness of the heart...

Our lips touch lightly. Our breathing becomes more pronounced. Finally a soft kiss followed by a more passionate one. With my eyes closed I put all my senses into perceiving this moment, this reality that my mind presents me with. I do not want it to ever end, but I know that everything is perishable. I could draw a picture of us in the wet sand of the shore, but the waves would hasten to erase it because the sand does not understand that memories can be kept. The beach is the place where nothing is remembered, where nothing is filed. Everything fades subtly caressed by the waves, with the oxide of the water, with the corrosion of the salt. Equally, in the forest I could create a mural of leaves which read "I Love You", but the wind would blow impassively, gently sweeping the leaves, blurring the letters with which I promised you eternal love. Let all wars be over, all hatred be erased, all money be rotten...

For everything is perishable. Like the heat of our bodies, like the kisses that we share, like our hearts beating in sync by the closeness of our chests. Our whole reality is a minuscule instant, a badly taken photo of the now, which perishes, and becomes the past, the yesterday, a memory, to make way for the next moment, the future, tomorrow, the rest of our lives. And again we feel it intensely, as it will only last as long as it takes for time to advance. In the same manner, in another time scale, our very essence is also perishable. A few decades after dying in our physical body, our genes will be diluted in generations to come, the memory of our very existence will be blurred, even disappeared, for not even the carriers of the memories of us would still be alive; the people we established relationships with, the people we created strong bonds of friendship with, the people that touched us, and gave us a place, however small, within their hearts. Even our planet is doomed to perish. Ours is just another story amongst so many stories that have been and that will continue to be written, until mother Earth stops radiating warmth. Let us not deceive ourselves. Even beyond the solar system, the sky is also subject to this universal law of the perishable, and will one day be only dust from which new worlds will emerge, new life, new energy, new love. Let the liars fall silent, let those who kill cease to live...

THE DISTANCE

There are just a few hours left to start killing the distance, but the distance is no longer what it was. It is not governed by the same definitions nor by the same measurements. It is not even defined by the time we have been apart. Now the distance is infinite, for now it is not the space between two points because all that exists is just the origin.

There are but a few hours left to begin the return. However, the return does not resemble what it did before. It is not defined by the same expectations nor is it driven by the same encounters. I foolishly hope for the same arms and the same eyes to be waiting for me. I cannot imagine anything, as it does not matter what I find at the other end of the road.

There is only one night left to return to the world as it was before. But even that is not true: the before that I left behind died without leaving a single after.

Tomorrow, at dawn, I will set my navigator to take me home. I wonder if the display will show a message reminding me that it does not recognize the destination. I will then fix my eyes on the road knowing that it is not the destination that matters, but the drive, killing miles, looking straight ahead. Watching the minutes pass while the odometer brands more and more numbers. The music on the radio at full volume distracting my thoughts, making the road my only world.

I know, however, that in the end I will reach the place I once departed, leaving behind your tears and taking mine with me, breaking into pieces the pages of our history and sipping the bitterness in a glass of red wine; burning our house with the fire of a thousand hells; planting sorrows at every turn, suffering in silence. Biting my lip to not scream that I love you, that I've always loved you, and I am so sorry that it is all ending like this, without a reason, without an ending worthy of mentioning, opening wounds that should have never been opened.

And when I arrive, I will find you awake. Or at least I will find someone who looks like you, but with more pain, with a sorrow I never knew before, and with no tears left, for all her crying has only left rivers of salt that cannot host any life at all.

And I don't know if that someone will give me a hug, or if she will shyly gaze down with her hands in her pockets. I do not dare guess whether she has saved some kisses for me, or if her lips will pour out words of indifference. Nor do I know if our hearts will beat for each other, as they did before, when our chests join.

And if she is to hug me, I wonder if her skin will tingle, or if it has become the hug of a stranger; if we will make love with the passion of the lovers we were before our last goodbye.

Tomorrow when I depart, I will find a road more infinite than ever.

WE DIE

I always thought tragedy was something that happened to others, that I was invincible, indestructible, capable of trapping time in my clock, and making it tick according to my own will. I had never attempted to define the interval between the now and the then, nor to observe the scars that years gone by had left in my existence. Now time is real, and as I am aware of this, time becomes aware of me. For time waits for no one. Darkness is where the eyes cannot see.

I always thought that death was the zenith of life. Now I know I was wrong: life is that short period of time in which we accumulate death, until we have so much of it that we have no choice but to die. For we die a little every day, from the moment we are born. We die with each second that goes by; we die when we fall out of love; we die with every word that hurts us; we die with every kiss that dies, not given, on our lips; with every 'I love you' we do not say, with every embrace we could have shared had we not been so busy with our hands in our pockets, searching for impossible reasons to carry on. We die every time we waste a perfect moment; we die listening to the music of the centuries playing in the background, killing almanacs, painting gray hairs in our memory. We die when instead of searching for ourselves, we remain still, as if trying to understand the meaning of the search. We die without even knowing where we have been lost.

I always thought that clocks ticked only for other people. Now I wish I could make more time even if it was just to feel sadness. I am here in the now, filling the empty spaces with dysmorphic voids, understanding that all that the moment brings is correct, all that divagates has a meaning. It will always be too late, unless it is now.

I hope my death will leave behind an echo, a colour in the wind, a dent in the horizon. I will slow down my heart beats to feel less pain. My soul has done what it came to do, has learnt what it must, and now is free again to dance under the rain without getting soaked, resuming its path amongst the laughter...

Where would I be but in your arms?

WITHOUT YOU

Sitting on my throne, in the highest tower in my Castle of Solitude, I read again the words you wrote in your farewell letter blurred by the tears I cried that day. You left and took my bleeding heart with you. You left behind the scarcity of kisses that follows passion; the absence of caresses; the light behind the curtain. My whole life suddenly stood still, worthless and wasted. Sadness since sleeps by my side, stealing dreams every night. Forgetfulness has arrived to stay, and wakes me up when I roll in bed to the side that was yours. You have taught me the most infinite void, the sourest of absences that hurts from within, where the sorrow seeks refuge.

Since you left, indolence seems to gather dust in the corners of melancholy, from where the spiders stare at me with great pity. The breeze of your kisses, the essence of your tenderness floats still in the air. I feel now so alone in a life built by your side. Never was our house so immense. Ice and frost keep growing in my sheets. I can still hear the echo of your empty hangers in your now empty wardrobe.

Since you left I have not been the same person. Even the shadows from the street pass the windows rapidly, fugaciously, as if escaping from my reality. The peace I seek keeps eluding me in every corner. The Moon looks at me and stays silent, confuses me, loses me amongst the guiding stars. For I can find no solace. Since you left, everything reminds me of you: the walls of the house, every ornament you left behind, every silence not filled with you singing. Arriving home and not finding you waiting to embrace me, to kiss me, to talk about our day. The sounds I now hear in the silence are but wailings that call your name.

Someone told me recently I have lost my spirit, that I am not the same happy and shining person, that my smile has faded. Someone told me recently to look after myself, and resolve my troubles. For when you left you took with you a part of who I am.

When you first arrived you shaped in an instant the emptiness that was killing me from within. No one inhabited it, there were no names written in chalk, it belonged to nobody. It needed some plasters to cover the wounds that allowed in hurt and pain. You left some time ago, but you left part of your soul resting on the window sill. Now there are only spaces in which you are not, arms that cannot embrace, lips that cannot kiss.

Whoever fills that void will only be filling in for you. Your name will always be engraved on the corner that you owned in my heart, now a well of tears and sourness. Whoever fills that void will only be filling up a space that is yours. For this is how I now feel: alone and lost, with no plans or faith. It hurts so much not having you when I need you. I keep searching for a cause, for a quest, for a memory to fill with dreams the little box where I keep the future so I can smile and laugh again. I need to find the path to make me want to carry on; I need to find the reasons for the next three hundred summers.

Take good care. I wish you well.

MY GRAVE

Alone, lost and scared, I sail through the streets of infinite darkness. Captive in the prison of their curves, I long for every moment that you were mine. Trapped in this island where your kisses cannot reach, I whisper love songs for you. I pluck petals from daisies that always deny me your love. I look at my compass, and it still points to the south.

Cruel is your heart. The birds sang for you once but you mistook their songs for deceitful voices, and chose to ignore them. No longer do you tell me that you love me and my scarred soul is stabbed once again by the same dagger. No longer do I feel you near and all the words I am scared to hear return to the desolated corner where my consciousness agonizes.

I look in the mirror and in my eyes' reflection I see your sweet, sad, once longing face. Thirsty for your kisses, lost in this sour labyrinth full of whispers and screams, I keep seeking your scent, your embrace and your soul. No matter where the wind carries you, there I shall search. Then, when the magic of the senses forge into a single feeling, I will become matter in your arms.

You made me thrill with every kiss. Every beat of my heart craves your attention in your absence. You gazed at me, melting the ice castles that other eyes built within my soul. You kissed me, infusing potions of amnesia into my mind, and you made me madden. In my deepest anguish, I am still in love with you.

For I cry for you, and you know this. I fade into tears that evaporate into clouds that rain over the nothingness. All those tears I once cried for you are only salt today. All those flowers that were watered with my tears, withered having no reason to bloom. All the love we shared faded away, lost within the cruel darkness of distance. Even so, I want to continue crying, shattering into a silence, kissing the sorrow that devastates me, drowning the rage.

For my grave awaits. All that is left for me is to fill it with tears.

THE ABSENCE OF YOU

Saying that I am well would be lying to you, my love. Since you left I am a mess. When we speak on the phone, or when I send you letters, I only pretend to be happy so that I don't taint you with my sadness. I speak of my plans, my new projects... at the same time, I realise nothing is achievable without you.

Thus, days go by, stretched to the point of absurdity and monotony. I still cook for two and your portion is always wasted. Sometimes I feed it to the stray dogs in the street. They are by now used to this routine and impatiently await, looking at me with sorrow. I listen to the conversations between my insanity and the echo of your words that still remains, haunting the house.

Saying I do not miss your hugs would be deceiving you, my sweetheart. But I miss them, for they departed with you to sail seas of salt and blood; to lands so far away that not even my shadow, projected by the setting Sun, can touch the absence of you. Not even by standing on my tiptoes. I keep whispering sighs full of sadness that call out your name before dispersing into infinity. I search for shells on the shore like we used to. I cry silently, as if pretending not to, my tears further filling that ocean between us.

Saying that I do not long for your kisses would be dishonest, my little heart. Exchanging feelings with each other, telling secrets we already knew. As if each kiss was a dose of what we are made of, of what we feel for each other. Since you left, my lips have given up smiling. As if the only reason they existed was for kissing yours. For living without you is not the opposite of living with you, my love: living without you is living with the absence of your kisses.

This year was not foreseen on any calendar. The time that has passed until now is the closest to a whole eternity. A time so eternal that even my clock feels overwhelmed and mute before such magnitude. Every day I fight a duel with the almanac sheets: I make battle plans to kill them with a fatal blow. But regardless of how much I sharpen my scissors, it always takes me the same twenty four hours to win the struggle. For without you I am not living: without you all I do is wait.

The distance that separates us tortures me every day. Not feeling you near worsens, even more, the absence of you. I miss your touch, like silk fabric falling free, uncovering a beautiful marble figure; like a flag without the wind that shapes it, brushing withering creases. That is how I am in the absence of you.

I must be strong while I wait, but I have no strength left. The day you return, all the oceans will dry to bring you home, to lower the horizon and permit that our eyes meet sooner. Then the spell will be complete and you will return to where you belong, where all is not all without you; where the air is dense and hot when you don´t breathe it; where the rain is not refreshing if you're not there; where the Moon weeps every night for the absence of you and where the Sun rises every morning solely out of routine and habit; where my arms only embrace the void that you have left.

A PROMISE

Because I made you a promise, I left my dreams stored in the box where I keep my winter clothes. I wrapped in brown paper my watch, my guitar and my ink well, and I allowed tomorrow to follow its path.

Because I gave you my word, I filled my lips with kisses, my heart with heartbeats, my nights with dreams, my memory with memories of you. I have abandoned it all to stare into your eyes for however long this present eternity may last.

Because I swore tomorrow to you, I exchanged my songs for waking up with you; I bartered with the beats from your heart. I opened the curtains of our house to the new dawn and the new Sun. I planted odd petalled daisies and watered them with love and tenderness. I wrote lullabies so you could sleep on the melody, and I drew smiles on the lips of destiny.

Because you dragged me to the maelstrom of your kisses, I tore my map into a hundred pieces and I buried under the rainbow the compass that before you guided my course. I sought the warmth of your arms in the place from where the winds blow. I trained my wind vane to point towards the place where you lived.

Because I promised to love you forever, I allowed the spiders to build webs in the corners of what I lived before you, to bore the past and cover it with dust. I forbade my eyes to look back and my ears to hear anything that was not your charm. I abandoned the mirage of what it was to follow your steps towards wherever you wanted me to.

A KNOT IN MY THOUGHTS

I tied a knot in my thoughts to remember a sound that faded to oblivion in a cloud of dust. I could have forever stayed in that moment, demolishing the unbreakable ice walls I once built between my past and my now, segregating what had fallen from what had not, annihilating the shadows of yesterday that interfered with the present, shaking the sand from my shoes, closing my eyes tightly to be able to see clearer the memory of us when we were young, when we were beautiful. That time is now gone and replaced by maturity behind which old age is hiding behind which death awaits. I know whatever life I have left is just the time that it takes for a scythe to be sharpened.

In my unhappiness, I envy the fortune of the flower that blooms every spring, to later wither, to then later show off again its beauty a few months before summer comes. Destinies, at times, are connected in ways we cannot comprehend, until past and present merge into a flawless moment.

I much prefer darkness to shadows, for shadows can hide anything within their depth: a ghost from yesterday, a memory full of destructive emotions, a murderer who does not fear death and who is only followed by his own shadow. I prefer, a thousand times over, memory to forgetfulness, for a man without forgetfulness is doomed to sadness, and a man without memory is sentenced to forgetfulness, to being only the shell of what he could have been.

Like a wound covered with an old bandage, like a scar before stormy weather, like a tattoo faded by the passing of so much time, like a pain forever trapped in the place where tears are made. Like a dry river where the sorrow dies, where kisses reach not. Like a hurricane of seeds that will not sprout in any soil, like a vase of withered flowers, like a clock unable to tick the time that I am with you, like the occasions when we do not fuse into an embrace. A desperate heart will always seduce the mind.

MY DAUGHTER

My daughter's name is Amy and she makes me very proud, for she fills with happiness the streets that she walks and the places she visits. Amy is incapable of hating, and if you know her, a little piece of her will forever own a place in your heart. Her heart is full of little pieces of the people she loves. She is one of those people you know you will never forget, even if you just met her briefly; and all those fortunate enough to cross paths with her, experience a change in some aspect of their own lives or their dreams, and become better people. Amy is full of joy, blonde and tall, with brown eyes, like her mother.

It has been three years since I left, and I know she feels the greatest of sorrows. She sang me a song the day I departed. That day the Sun was bright and high in a clear blue sky, you could still see the Moon from the night before; butterflies were hovering randomly amongst the flowers, and birds started their migration towards the summer. It was as if the cosmos wanted to show the feelings I myself could not let out. She always made me proud when she sang. Sometimes, when we were together, she would make me cry with happiness with her songs. I have no doubt she loves me with all her soul and I know she really misses me.

She talks to me every day: she tells me she is sad and everything reminds her of me; she tells me she has lost her smile, and that it is not fair I had to go. She sees me all around her, almost obsessively: such is her nostalgia.

Recently while she was walking the dog, a sparrow flew around her and softly landed on her arm. She caressed it for a little while and then extended her arm inviting it to fly, but instead, it glided to the ground and started moving in little jumps around her. The dog, completely uninterested in catching it, just laid on the grass, wagging its tail, following the little sparrow with its gaze. Amy thought that perhaps the sparrow was bringing her a message from me, something to whisper in her ear.

She speaks constantly of me, for everything, as I said, reminds her of me. I regret to see that she lives in a memory, in a time now gone, because when she remembers our shared happiness she is just digging deep holes in the path to her own happiness. Perhaps the sparrow wanted to tell her that it is time to let go. She must rejoice in the moments and the laughter we shared, the love we gave to each other that still lives on, even now when I am not there. Crying is futile, although I understand only rocks can remain immutable when a loved one goes away. Seeking answers will lead to nowhere, trying to understand that which has no explanation is like trying to make sense out of madness. It is much better to give in, to let go of what we didn't have time to do, to stop thinking of how unfair life can sometimes be.

I know she cries at night, when no one sees her. She cries for me, for the absence of me, wishing she could have just one more cuddle. I did everything I could for her when we were together. I taught her to respect others and to be compassionate. I did not have enough time to teach her to be happy, to enjoy every day as if it was the last but one, to admire the beauty of our Universe, to live with passion. I only managed to show her the way, hoping that by my example she would reach a state of calm, of inner peace, of empathy for all those who suffer.

As for me, I am trapped in this permanent uncomfortable state, of eternal agony and infinite pain that lets me not fulfill my destiny. Like a doubt that reaches no conclusion; like a poem half written. I hover between two worlds, wishing my daughter could let me go. I wish she could just remember fondly what we had and could forget the sorrow of what will never be again

Not long ago, I sent her another message with a white butterfly, and this time she understood. Now she remembers me as we were before

I departed, when we were together. She has finally buried the sadness, she has opened her eyes again to the present and to the future, thus setting me free.

I let her know that I was at last free from the chains of suffering and I became the sunsets, the movement of the tides, the blossoming flowers, the light of the distant stars. I let her know in a way that she would at last understand. When she became aware of it, she stood still and cried happy tears. The breeze carried from the distance the song she sang at my funeral.

THE CRUISE SHIP

Life onboard a cruise ship is like life in a small town. The ship is divided into crew and passenger areas. Each one is fully independent in the way that it works. Both of these areas have their own canteen, gym, cabins... Just like small neighbourhoods, the maze of corridors resembles a small floating community. Here onboard the ship we all know each other, the main difference with society on land being that we all work for a common goal and we all depend on each other. There is no democracy but there is no tyranny either. It is an understanding higher than all that, beyond social systems and death penalties.

The outer world is a kind of illusion. Every day you wake up at a new port, a new city, a new country. Sometimes, when we cross an ocean, we spend several days in deep sea surrounded only by water, wind and sunsets made of colours that are not possible inland. This is our only universe.

Beyond the horizon lays the limit to another dimension. Beyond the horizon there are infinite possibilities to explain reality. Like wondering with your eyes closed what you will find when you open them, everything that has been and everything that will be awaits behind that unreachable line where the sky kisses the sea. Most of the time you cannot find your location on a map, but that is not important, unless you work on the navigational bridge.

News from the outside world, that world that we know exists but can only dream of, arrives through different channels. You cannot buy your favourite paper, and you cannot choose your favourite news program. There is only one TV news channel and, most of the time, satellite signal is so poor that it is impossible to follow. Even when reception is good, the news is all the same anyway: so many deaths here, so many wounded there, the stock market is collapsing, and with it, the bank you have trusted your savings to... You switch off the TV swearing never to switch it on again. You realise that you are far happier in ignorance, neglecting the outside world, just believing that everything is alright out there, without the hurt of knowing the news. This kind of ignorance, this absence of utility bills and phone calls from a perseverant seller, is in itself one of the many shapes of happiness.

Thus, the days go by, with great calm and ease. You wake up in the morning and go to work. Then you have a coffee and socialise, most of the time with other crew members, sometimes with passengers. Occasionally you become closer to some of the passengers you socialise with, who like adventurous travellers in a strange land, bring stories, messages of that outer world that exists beyond the sea, in our hopes and dreams. Lunch is another opportunity to socialise. As you can see, there are many of these opportunities in this isolated world. You go to work again in the afternoon, and in the evening you can go see the shows, the cabaret, or just to have a non alcoholic drink with the musicians, the artists or some passenger you share a table with.

The most abundant thing is time. That precious commodity in land is found everywhere here, in every corner. Wherever you seek, you will find time, unhurried, eternal, and not boring at all. And you can spend it however you want: learning whatever you set your mind to; thinking of the thousands of reasons for everything, for every conclusion; playing with entangled hallucinations; listening to the birds telling their stories; studying meticulously the path the clouds follow; observing the seagulls showing off their gliding skills, guiding us to land. Or simply to exercise the power of the mind, seeking answers beyond the answers, beyond reason and madness. For everything is beautiful and in harmony. All begins and ends with you. All is possible and at the same time a dream. All is you.

When you live onboard a cruise ship it is easy to forgive. When you live onboard it is easy to forget your past, your life in that society where people that are not sailors live. Letting yourself be dragged by today, mattering not which port we will arrive in tomorrow, the day after, or in a week's time. For the destination is not important: it is only important to sail, cross the mysterious waters that fill the abyss, swing on the waves, admire the sunsets looking for stray dolphins, migrating whales or floating icebergs. Forgetfulness invades everything, even the love you left behind. That love that was so missed at the start of the journey is somehow diluted by the salty air, the calm of the sea, the stars in the night sky, until it becomes something so distant, a thought you are not sure of, a reality that will be mistaken for a dream upon waking. For it is easy to mix true feelings with hopes; it is easy to understand how love can start a new flame, effortlessly, just by letting yourself go, regardless of promises made, or how much we might want to fight it. For when you live onboard a cruise ship, the only reality is the present, the now and the I, and everything that once was is left behind.

YOUR SILENCE

It is your silence my love, a curtain of air that fills the eternal distance that separates us. The infinite void that occupies the space where words used to be, absorbing the sound to engrave it in granite tombstones. Your silence is the singularity that contracts the cosmos, only to let it expand again, burning the oxygen, heralding the asphyxia, furthering us even more from that moment where embraced we belong together. The withered smell of reproach is what disintegrates my soul and rips from my face the mask that looks back at me from the ground, delivering ruthlessly my doubts to the dessert of exile.

It is your silence my dear, the horizon where time stands still, where the Moon awaits your words to regain movement. It is the universe where all the battles that were once lost are hidden. It is where the air once exhaled from your lungs seeks refuge. It is your silence, the assassin of my poems, the flame that burns the staves of all the songs I could never write. It is that absence that makes me long to hear even what I would rather not, as long as you end this eternity so full of nothing. It is your silence the barren echo that bounces amongst the four walls of my desolation; the space where the words we said to each other can still be heard; the ocean where my questions struggle to reach your ears, sinking at every attempt.

It is your silence my sweetheart, the fright that does not allow me to cry. It is the ghost of your thoughts floating morbidly in the ether; your way of describing this moment with no sound. It is your silence, the intangible wall, the barbed wire that keeps away all that we could say to each other. It is the indifference in your gaze when your motionless lips fail to shape your breath into meaning. It is your silence, the arid desert with no perfume, the daisy with no petals that says nothing. It is your silent voice, the dagger that rips my chest when it goes beyond the end of eternity.

It is your silence, my love, that figure in the dark that needs light to reveal its shape. It is the mute and frightening shriek that can only be heard, when you do not speak, by those used to the sound of your voice. It is the windless storm that disturbs the warm sandy shores. The acid rain that will leave behind lifeless poppy fields. It is that open door that lets in everything we denied into existence. It is everything that is not real, stretched into an eternity; the scythe that slices my words into syllables, detaching them from their meaning. It is that music with no sound that transmits so much.

It is your silence, the annihilating force that makes the air heavier, that cannot be defeated by the kisses I throw at you. It is your silence, the sound that is not heard until it ceases to exist. It is the absence of words that returns pretending never to have departed. It is the code that decrypts all the other silences. This lack of words, of wailings, of laughter, it is to me a crown of thorns that dig into my skin to rip away pieces of flesh, leaving behind a poison that does not kill, but sentences to endless doubt.

Silence might be the absence of sound.

Your silence, nevertheless, is the absence of everything.

SHOOTING STARS

I met her in spring time, on the exact same day that every flower bloomed in an incomparable beautiful choreography. Last night´s Moon was still visible in the sky, and the only cloud that gave us shade was shaped like a heart. The smell of jasmine had the colours of the rainbow and the music of Triana; and there we were, the two of us, witnesses of this unique moment. With our eyes closed, we took in slow deep breaths and, in my mind, the smell of spring filled the air and everything. As I opened my eyes I saw her, as if she had appeared out of nowhere, my destiny staring back at me.

At first I thought we had never met before, but after just one moment I was certain we had shared many lives together. I had seen her eyes in the constellation of Sagittarius, in every clear night´s sky; I had seen her face in all the petals that said "she loves me"; I had witnessed the waves gently rocking her to sleep at every sunset. When she told me her name, three white butterflies fluttered gracefully out of her mouth, hovered all around us for an instant, and departed decidedly, for the horizon. An echo repeated her name to engrave it in my memory. Her name was María.

We started to walk together and, as we turned the corner, we held each other's hands. At that very moment time stood still, and we spent several eternities looking into each other's eyes. When no secrets were left untold, we drew a heart with chalk, wrote our names inside, and decided to allow time to continue.

At the very first second of this new era we were transported to a poppy field where we ran free amongst a constellation of Pegasi. The Sorrow, pursuing us in the form of a dense grey fog, was abandoned miles away and unable to regain its breath. Ahead of us the horizon, crowned by a rainbow of flowers inhabited by gatherings of fairies from Neverland. Legend had it that happiness could be sought after closer than where the eyes reach.

In the blink of an eye we were conveyed to a candle lit room, where we tenderly held onto one another. From our gentle touch, sparks escaped through the window, flying up like shooting stars to decorate the night's sky. As we kissed, a star came before us and fell gracefully next to us. I took it in my hand and gave it to María.

We dissolved into a cloud of tenderness, and together we travelled through millions of galaxies on a journey many light-years long. Our pure radiant love illuminated the Universe leaving a glow over our trail, and that very same love was creating new life. As we crossed the entrance into a new dimension, we metamorphosed into matter again, to continue our timeless journey towards infinity.